The Idiot

by

Errol Dawson

Cover illustration by Terry Fitzgibbon

www.makingwaves.co.nz

EXTRACT
HOUSE

The Idiot © 2009 Errol Dawson

This edition published 2013
ISBN-13: 978-1492160304
ISBN-10: 149216030X

From the Author

Whether you pester somebody to read this book to you, or you read it to yourself, I feel sure you will like the Idiot, and the strange thoughts that enter his head.

I would also like you to know that this is not an autobiography. For one thing, I am nowhere near as clever/stupid as the Idiot, nor as brave.

But I did marry a princess, and although I don't live in a castle, I do have two sons who have often enjoyed going on the Idiot's journey with me.

It is a journey of discovery...

EXTRACT
HOUSE

Illustration Credits

for

Blake + Myles

enough for me to buy some jam,' he thought. And it wasn't far away. So he left the road and scrambled after it.

He soon found himself climbing over fences, sloshing through soggy ditches and overcoming all sorts of obstacles to get to the rainbow. Bushes, brambles, bracken, and low hanging branches barred his way and scratched him as he battled through them. The further from the road he ventured the wilder the countryside became. Finally, he found the rainbow lurking in a clearing.

"Ah-ha," he cried, as he jumped out from behind a bush, "now I've got you!" But it was no longer there! He looked frantically about him, until he saw it shimmering in the distance behind a hill. He scrambled after it again.

The same thing happened, and again. Every time he reached the place where the rainbow was, only to find it had moved to somewhere else. Eventually, the Idiot grew weary. "I'm not playing this game with you anymore, Rainbow," he loudly declared.

It was then that he remembered why he was chasing after the rainbow in the first place. Of course, by now he was hopelessly lost and had no idea in what direction the shop might be.

"I wish I wasn't so hungry," he said to himself.

"Grrrruurruubrrruuup," his stomach answered.

Witch Way

Then, just like it fell from the sky, an idea struck him. 'If I can't find the shop, maybe I can get the shop to come to me.' So the Idiot jumped up and down on the spot shouting "Yaay, shop, I'm over here. Come to me shop. Bring me something to eat pleeeze." But no matter how high he jumped or how furiously he waved his umbrella, the shop did not come.

He was ready to give up and go home when he saw a little old lady hobbling towards him. She was whistling a strange tune. As she drew near she stopped whistling and spoke to him in a sweet, kind voice. "Why, whatever is all the commotion about? Why are you shouting and waving and jumping about like a blithering idiot?" she asked.

So the Idiot told her.

"Dear, oh dear," said the little old lady, "You won't get the shop to come to you."

"Why not?" he asked.

"I would have thought that was obvious," replied the little old lady. "Shops can't keep running from one person to another; that would take too long and make them too tired. No, that's not how it works at all. The shop doesn't go to you; you have to go to it."

"But I don't know where it is," said the Idiot.

"Don't you dear? Well, perhaps I can help you. Just beyond that hill over there;" she pointed the way with a crooked and gnarled finger, "is a waterfall, and beyond the waterfall is a tunnel, and beyond the tunnel... is the shop!"

"That must be why I couldn't find it;" he cried excitedly, "it was hiding!" Then he shouted out, "here I come, shop, ready or not!"

The little old lady watched, as he scampered away up the hill, and began to laugh. But her chuckle soon became a cackle. It echoed around the hills becoming louder and more menacing. Then, in one swift movement, she spun around, threw her cloak about her, and disappeared!

Meanwhile, the Idiot reached the top of the hill and ran down the other side. Suddenly, he stopped. He could go no further; for rising up before him were great rocky cliffs that stretched away on either side, as far as he could see, forming a giant impenetrable wall. There was no way he was going to get over or around it. But there was also, right in front of him, just as the old lady predicted, a waterfall.

It tumbled over the rocks high above the Idiot's head into a shallow pool at his feet. He walked towards the falling water, using rocks as stepping stones, holding his opened umbrella. Suddenly, he noticed something odd; as he passed under the waterfall he remained dry! It was like being in a glass bubble in the middle of a thunder storm.

Water pounded his umbrella, and was smashed into a million drops by rocks that were being polished and made slippery, by the constantly falling water. He took care not to let his feet

slide out from under him. Soon they found dry ground again and the noise on his umbrella stopped.

He was no longer under the waterfall; instead, he found himself in a small cave behind it. Above him, the overhanging cliff formed a roof and there were rocky walls on three sides. It was like being in a small room with water, instead of glass, as a window. He also noticed a large crack in the rock to his right.

It was just big enough for him to get through, although it was a tight squeeze. Just as well he hadn't eaten breakfast, otherwise he probably wouldn't have managed it; as it was he had to hold his breath and suck in his stomach.

Suddenly, he was in a dark, damp tunnel.

Tunnel

The loud splashing of the waterfall was now a hushed whisper. He could hear the drip, drip of single drops as they splattered onto wet ground or plopped into puddles. His footsteps sloshed loudly in the eerily quiet tunnel. So did other footsteps behind him.

Wait! What was that? Was someone else there? He stopped and listened. Nothing! He looked over his shoulder; he saw no-one.

As his eyes grew accustomed to the dark, he began to see vague shapes about him. He could just make out the brickwork of the tunnel walls and the curved roof, but there was still plenty of darkness in which someone could hide. He walked forward again. Once more, there was the sound of other footsteps behind him. He spun around. This time, he saw something.

Two giant, luminous eyes glowered down at him and a luminous mouth with jagged teeth snarled. The monster, for that is what it surely was, made no sound; nor did it move. The Idiot was not stupid enough to wait for it to do so, but as he turned around to run away, he slipped and fell to the ground.

He had no choice but to lie as still as possible. With a bit of luck, the monster would pass over him without knowing where he was.

He closed his eyes, and lay as quiet as a sleeping mouse with laryngitis.

Nothing happened.

He opened his eyes. The monster was still bearing down upon him but, strangely, the Idiot was no longer afraid. It could easily have eaten him, or done something equally despicable, if it had wanted to. Maybe it just wanted to be friends. He got to his feet.

"Hello," the Idiot said, but to no reply. The eyes didn't blink, and the mouth had the same crooked snarl as before.

Cautiously, he went over to it. Still it did not move. Being careful not to put his hand anywhere near its teeth, he poked the big monster somewhere where he thought its belly ought to have been. But his finger touched the wall of the tunnel instead. Still the eyes did not blink, nor

the mouth move. He put the palms of both of his hands on the wall of the tunnel, and moved them over its surface. Nothing stirred. It was when he poked the monster's eyes with his fingers that he realized it was no monster at all.

The wall of the tunnel was slimy where he thought the eyes and teeth had been. Water had leaked in from outside and formed damp patches on the bricks. Then the moss had come, the greasy, icky moss that looked fluorescent in the little light that was in the tunnel, which gave it a spooky, luminous quality. "Well, I'm glad you're not a monster," the Idiot said to the moss as he backed away. The moss did not answer.

He trudged on again, but made up his mind not to be frightened by anything else in the tunnel. Even when the other footsteps started up again, he ignored them. To stop from being scared, he began whistling a tune. He did not know what tune it was, until he remembered that he had heard the kind old lady whistle it on the other side of the waterfall. He was surprised that he remembered it.

As the Idiot made steady progress down the tunnel, he noticed a small peephole of light in front of him. The more he walked towards it, the bigger it grew. He could see the outside again and knew that he would soon be in it. So he ran, making the circle of light get bigger quicker. He heard the other footsteps running behind him, but he ignored them. Before he knew it, the hole was bigger than he was, and he went from underground night to be surrounded by daylight once more. As soon as he did so, the other footsteps stopped.

I don't know whether the Idiot realized the other footsteps were merely echoes of his own, or whether, even to this day, he thinks that they belonged to a tunnel dwelling creature that follows people around in the dark.

Whatever he thought, he put it out of his mind, for he knew his journey to the shop would soon be over, and he was looking forward to some breakfast. He hoped his stomach, which gguurrrumped in anticipation would forgive him for taking so long.

He soon became aware, however, that the countryside here was not the same as he usually passed by on the way to the shop.

It was a barren scene which greeted him now: brown tussock grasses and rocks and weeds as far as the eye could see. There were no flowers anywhere, but spindly, leafless trees sparsely peppered the alien looking landscape. At least a

clear path wound its way through it, so onward he went.

It wasn't long before a building came into view. Was that the shop? Somehow, he just knew it wasn't.

This was a castle!

He found himself in a large, empty hall, with a vaulted, arched roof that echoed the slightest of sounds. Even his breathing was repeated back at him like a thousand whispers. Because he couldn't think of anything else to do, the Idiot collapsed his umbrella. 'This place is umbriferous enough,' he thought; 'besides, there aren't any birds in here either.'

Suddenly, the sounds of rattling and clanking chains rang loud in his ears. He turned in time to see the drawbridge rising up. In an instant, he knew that if he didn't run back he may never get out. In a great burst of speed he raced onto the bridge, but the harder and faster he ran the steeper it became.

He passed the half-way point quite quickly but the slope became too steep and his feet began to skid. Somehow he clambered his way to the top. But the drawbridge was now too high for him to jump from, and to make the top of the cliff on the other side of the great chasm. Even as he thought about doing so, the distance was increasing. He had no choice but to slide back down. He landed with a thud back inside the castle. With a final clang, the great drawbridge locked itself into place and everything became black.

'That's not fair', he thought. 'It's not dark-time yet!' He then turned his thinking to his predicament. How might he get out of this dreadful place which was obviously not a shop?

'I suppose castles have back doors, just like regular homes,' he figured. So, with a shrug, he wandered deeper into the dark, to look for one.

There was no hope of finding anything or anyone in that great, big, dark, echoing place. He couldn't even see his hand in front of his face.

When he banged into a wall, making a 'donk' sound, he decided that walking around with his hand in front of his face was *not* a good idea.

He felt his way forward, as if playing 'blind man's bluff': touching the air or walls that appeared before him, not knowing in which direction he needed to go. Passageways opened up before his hands, and he travelled down them one by one. But he always found himself back in the same large hall.

He had never felt so alone. He hadn't seen a single living thing since he had left the tunnel. And he noticed now, for the first time, how deathly quiet was this strange land. No sound of chirping birds had entered his ears, no dogs barked, not even the dull hum of distant traffic hinted at a busy life beyond the castle walls. The only sounds he could hear came from himself.

His heart-beat and his breathing were much more noticeable, now that their only competition for the attention of his ears was silence. Then, of course, not to be out-done, there was his stomach. It roared loudly, echoing around the walls again and again, so that it sounded like several ravenous, growling beasts.

Feeling utterly wretched and angry, he

stopped where he was and shouted out. "All I want is something to eat and to get back home. Is that too much to ask?"

"Something to eat, get back, eat, home, something to eat, ask, get back home, too much, too much to ask, ask, ask..." he answered himself in echoing reply.

His voices were not the only sounds he heard.

Bells + Spells

The Idiot was back in the same hallway with many hallways leading off it, but he was too impatient to try them all again. Instead, he just stood there and held up his little lantern, looking about him and wondering what else he could do.

It was then that he saw the ropes, four of them, dangling from the roof far above. He could not resist giving the first one a strong pull. "Dong!" Loud and echoing came back the sound of a big, brass bell from somewhere high up in the castle. He gave the next one a pull. This one was higher in tone... "dung." The third was higher again... "dang." The fourth note was even higher still... "ding."

"Well that's gone and done it," said the Idiot to himself. "If that witch is anywhere within a hundred miles of this place, I sure hope she's deaf". But there was something irresistible about pulling the ropes and making the bells ring. He kept pulling at them in different sequences, making up different tunes.

This was fun! It was so much fun that he completely forgot why he was there. But what did manage to come into his head was the

strange tune he had heard the Witch whistle, right back when he thought that she was a kind old lady. He tried to re-create the tune by pulling on the ropes in the correct order. There were fifteen notes in all. He had to pull the first rope first, the fourth rope second; the second rope third, the third rope fourth, and so on. Then something strange happened.

The Idiot heard what sounded like grinding rock while, in the middle of the hall, the floor began to rise up, taking the shape of a great spiral staircase.

The Idiot watched fascinated. He didn't think to jump onto it as it rose steadily upwards. If he did, he would have saved himself a long climb. Instead, he squinted at the stairs as they twisted and spiraled higher and higher. In the dim light his eyes saw the topmost steps finally come to rest outside a door at the highest point in the tower. 'That must be where the Princess is', he thought. 'I'd better go and rescue her'.

So he jumped onto the staircase and began to climb. In all, he had to climb five hundred and thirty seven stairs, but the Idiot lost count after ten.

The air about him grew darker and gloomier the higher he went. The floor became a shadow below. The staircase had no handrail, and was getting narrower the higher he went. Then it began to move!

It was like being on the long neck of some serpentine monster, that kept turning around on itself to find him. It was difficult to know where to put his feet without stepping into thin air! He leaned forward to hang on to the stairs, but with the umbrella in one hand and the lantern in the other, he couldn't. He had to drop one of them.

He chose to let the lantern go and watched its glow get swallowed by the darkness. When it finally hit the ground and smashed, a tiny fireball flared up for a moment, then darkness again. With one hand now free, and using the umbrella as a walking stick to steady himself, he clambered on up the stairs.

Then there came to his ears a terrible shrieking cackle. It echoed around the tower and came back at him again and again. He knew that, somehow, the Witch could see him and was laughing at his feeble attempts. He couldn't put his hands over his ears because they were busy. All he could do was to grit his teeth and go on.

As the stairs swayed and turned, the Idiot began to feel sick. It took every effort just to hang on, and to keep his legs pushing himself upwards. He had no idea how much higher he had to go. All he knew was, if he fell, it was a long way down.

Then, came the bats!

Bat Attack

At first they were just a few dark shadows that appeared in the gloom about him. But more and more of them gathered. They flew around him; then they dove at him, beating down upon him in relentless waves, then swerving away, only to come back and dive at him again.

The bats shrieked and squealed, using their clever ears to read echoes, just as you or I might use our eyes to read a map. The closer they got, the bolder they became, until they were clawing him with their sharp talons. The more the Idiot tried to shoo them away the more unsteady he became. But if he did nothing, their claws shredded his clothes and cut his skin.

"Aaaarrrgh," he screamed, as he beat off yet another attack, and then scrambled up higher as quick as he could.

It was then he noticed something that gave him hope. The bats couldn't find him! As they came in for another attack, they went lower down the stairs, to where he had been when he screamed. All too soon, though, they found him again. So he screamed again, and clambered up the stairs once more.

The Idiot didn't know that bats use their ears and not their eyes to find out where things are. He just kept screaming and climbing out of the way, which confused their sensitive ears. By the time they had gone to where the Idiot was when he screamed, he was somewhere else. In this way he made good progress up the stairs. Finally, exhausted, dizzy and bleeding, he made it to the topmost step. He was facing the door at the top of the tower. Carefully, he opened it.

Immediately, a strong gust of wind blew in at him from outside, nearly toppling him backwards down the stairs.

Brilliant daylight blazed into his eyes.

Bridge

The Idiot had the good sense to stand where he was, and wait until his eyes became accustomed to the light. For beyond the door there was no floor. There was nothing but the most slender of bridges.

This was not the sort of bridge that you and I are used to. It had no safety rail, and was only one foot wide.

At the other end was another tower, the same height as the one he had just left. It had a pink door with a gold 'P' in the middle.

'Maybe that's where the Princess is,' the Idiot

thought. Without hesitation, he stepped onto the bridge and began to walk carefully across it.

He felt the wind rush about him, as if it were trying to knock him over the edge. He looked down; all he could see, far below, were clouds and flying birds. By the time he was half way across, he was dizzy with fear and swaying dangerously. He decided it would be safer to keep both feet on the bridge instead and slide, rather than walk, the rest of the way.

He put one foot forward, then slid the other foot behind to meet it. He repeated this

movement, over and over, all the while using his arms for balance. Later on, when the Idiot became famous, this sliding, swaying step became a popular type of dance.

Finally, he was across the bridge and knocking on the pink door.

"Princess! Are you there Princess?"

The door creaked open, and there, on the threshold, was a very pretty lady with long, fair hair. She had a slim face and a cute, pert nose.

"Princess?" the Idiot asked.

"Oh, how wonderful," she said, clapping her hands, "At long last, you've come to save me. Come in, come in."

"Um, I don't think I should," the Idiot replied. "We should leave here right away. That Witch is somewhere hereabouts. She can cast some really mean spells, and I don't want it to take a month for me to get to the toilet!"

"Oh, no," said the lady, "I'm sure I can come up with something better than that for you!"

But the Idiot didn't notice what she had said, or the harshness that was creeping into her voice. "Come on Princess, follow me," he cried and sprang back onto the bridge.

"But you can't go that way," she laughed. Suddenly, something strange happened.

The bridge was no longer made of solid rock. It was turning into a kind of gooey quicksand on which he could no longer walk. His feet sank deep into it and poked out underneath. He turned to go back, but each step took him further through the bridge. He was in serious danger of falling through it completely, down to the rocks far below. So he did what any idiot would do. He lay down and started to swim.

This was better, but he made slow progress. It was hard work trying to swim through thick, gooey rock, especially with an umbrella in one hand. But even as he neared the end of the bridge, it turned into dry sand. He had just enough time to throw himself onto the threshold of the tower. He hauled himself up until he was standing inside the doorway once more.

It was no lady that stood before him now, but an old crone, who no longer tried to disguise her voice. She laughed mercilessly. Her laughter beat upon his ears like short, staccato screams.

The bridge dissolved completely into sand and, even as the Idiot watched, the wind blew it into a swirling cloud that vanished into the space between the two towers. There was no going back that way.

The old crone roughly grabbed the Idiot by his jacket, and dragged him inside.

"Come on," she crowed, "I know another way."

princess?

Coming slowly to the Idiot, was the thought that things were not as they seemed. For one thing, this princess didn't look like, well, a princess. Now that he was up close to her, he could see that her hair was dirty and matted. As you know, real princesses brush their hair three thousand and twenty-seven times every day, but this hag's hair looked as though it had *never* been brushed, or washed.

Then there was her nose. It no longer looked pert or cute. He could see now that it was sharp and pointy, and had a hairy wart on its tip.

Her clothes too were another tell-tale sign. The Idiot thought, quite rightly too, that any self-respecting princess should be dressed in the finest of long, flowing silk gowns, richly embroidered with jewels and gold. But this old crone wore a tattered dress with roughly stitched patches. Below the dress, knobby knees poked out from skinny, hairy legs. Then there were the boots. They were not the slender slippers that princesses normally wore. These were the ugliest pair of holey, hob-nailed boots you could imagine.

"You're not a princess!" he accused.

She renewed her dry, screeching laugh, which made the Idiot's blood shiver inside him. She clapped her hands, and the door slammed shut.

In that small room at the top of the tower he didn't need his eyes to tell him where she was. She stank like rotten fish. First, he stuck fingers up his nose, to block out the smell, but then he had to open his mouth to breathe. This was no better, because he could now *taste* the smell of her. All the while she was getting closer and closer. The Idiot backed away until he felt the wall behind him.

He watched in horror as she raised her wand of terrible power and, in a low, threatening voice, began an incantation:

Something here smells worse than fear.
More than any nose can bear.
Something you want to run away from.
Everyone both far and near.
My stinky, rotten, smelly bum!

When she said the last word she hit the air with her wand, turned her back to the Idiot, poked out her bum, and farted.

The Idiot fainted from the smell.

Ring of Fire

When he awoke, he was surrounded by trees. It was deep night. He lay on his back looking skyward. Through tangled branches he could see at least a million stars overhead, but he lost count after ten.

For a moment, he thought he was back home, for he would often go to sleep out of doors looking up at the stars, without a blanket or a pillow, when he accidently locked himself out of his house. All too soon he remembered, with a sickening dread, he was far from home.

He sat up and looked about him. The Witch

was nowhere to be seen. But he did notice a strange, yellow light coming from somewhere; it was not the pale light of the moon that shone overhead, turning the trees into ghostly outlines; it was a dappled light, like the reflection of sun on a moving river, bathing everything it touched in golden hues -trees, grass, even the Idiot.

He looked about him. Through the trees, in a clearing, he saw the cause of the strange fluttering light: a large ring of fire. He stood up and walked towards it, getting warmer the nearer he got. The flames flared up fiercely at

his approach, stopping him from entering the ring, which he really wanted to do, because he saw something inside it that made his heart beat faster.

In the middle of the ring of fire was a slab of stone; and on that stone was a soft velvet mattress, and on that mattress was a princess.

I know what you are thinking; she's probably just another witch. But no, the Idiot could see her very clearly between the flickering flames. She wore what princesses were supposed to wear. Her gown was made of golden silk. Her delicate legs were smooth with no wiry hairs in sight, and elegant, blue slippers hugged her slender feet. Her skin was smooth and very un-witch-like. Her hair was as silken as her dress, and there were no warts anywhere.

At first glance, the Idiot thought that she must be dead and his heart sank; for she was pale and did not move, and her eyes were closed. Still, he could not believe it, would not believe it.

He wanted to leap heroically through the flames, scoop her up in his arms, and carry her far away. He tried running at the fire, but it defeated him. Every time he approached, the flames flared up to twice his height. Around and around he went, looking for a weak point in the ring: a place where the fire was not as intense. Again and again he charged at it. Each time he was beaten back by the heat.

He knew that the ring of fire was a magic one, because trees, grass, and earth all remained untouched by the flames. But were he to try and

pass through them, the Idiot knew only too well, he would not escape being turned into ash. He had to try something, but he had no idea what.

"So, Mr. Hero, what are you going to do now?"

The Witch was suddenly beside him. The Idiot was too surprised to answer.

"Well?" she asked again.

"Well what?" asked the Idiot in return.

"Aren't you going to save her?" she mocked.

"Er, I guess."

"What are you waiting for, an invitation?"

The Idiot looked at the trapped princess. He thought also of the poor, shuffling people and the spell that this witch had put on them. He didn't want something similar to happen to him. But neither was he going to give up.

"I *am* going to save her," said the Idiot, in a loud, clear voice. And he suddenly realized that he was not afraid.

"Hahahahahaha," she cackled. "And just how do you suppose you are going to do that?"

"With this," he said, brandishing his umbrella.

The Witch broke into her most dreadful, side-splitting cackle.

"And what, pray, is that?"

"My wand," said the Idiot.

The Witch stopped laughing. It was the strangest wand she had ever seen. Quickly, he made the umbrella spring open in her face. She got such a shock that she fell backwards.

You know, there aren't many good things that can be said of witches, but one of them is that they don't know what an umbrella is. They have no need of them; they just cast a spell and it stops raining.

So, while the Witch was dumbfounded, the Idiot closed his eyes and rushed at the flames, holding his umbrella as a shield. Fire flared up and burned the umbrella's canopy, leaving only its metal struts and handle undamaged. He felt heat all over him, like an oven door had just been opened. Flames singed his hair and clothes. He fell backwards, head over heels from the onslaught of the fierce blaze.

"So, any more bright ideas?" the Witch mocked, standing uncomfortably close to him once more. He tried not to breath in her stink.

"Maybe I can be of some assistance," she surprisingly offered. At first the Idiot was skeptical; he knew she had to be up to no good. But he really wanted to save the princess.

"But how are we going to get through the ring of fire to save her?" he asked.

"Oh, you're not going *through* the flames," she answered. "Follow me," and she led the way through the forest to one particular tree.

The Idiot didn't realize that the Witch had selected this tree because it was neither too old and stiff, nor too young and flimsy. In tree terms it was probably a teenager, and it was both strong and flexible.

The old Witch jiggled it back and forth to test it. "This will do nicely," she croaked. Even though it was not quite all grown up, it was still a tall tree, and towered above their heads. She pulled it down towards herself with a strength that amazed the Idiot. Her arms grew bigger and bigger, instantly growing bulging muscles that had not been there before. The tree creaked and groaned in protest, at the strain it was being put under, as the Witch ran her hands along its length, all the while pulling it down until, finally, the top of the tree was nearly touching the ground.

"I don't get it," the Idiot said in his low, slow voice. "How is this going to help the princess?"

"You'll see," she replied mysteriously. "Here, hold this." Without thinking, the Idiot grabbed hold of the tree at its tip. Then, without warning, the Witch let it go.

The tree sprang back up, dragging the Idiot with it, catapulting him high in the air. He somersaulted like a rugby ball, turning end over end. Instead of tumbling over goal posts, however, he sailed high over the ring of fire.

Flames leaped up and licked at him, but he was flying too high and too quick. Then he was falling. Down, down he dropped, eventually landing inside the ring of fire. He made a big dent in the hard ground. The wind was knocked out of him, and he lay for a minute gasping for air.

Once he got his breath back he felt the pain. It was his body's way of saying 'what did you have to do that for?' Then, his arms, legs, head and butt all argued amongst themselves as to which of them was in more agony. His butt won; it was a good few days before he could sit on it without wincing. At least he was inside the ring of fire. But he soon wished he wasn't.

He had no way of getting out and no idea about what to do next.

Amulet

He slowly got to his feet and limped over to where the princess lay. She was even more beautiful close-up. Her skin was flawlessly smooth, and every strand of her hair shimmered like gold.

As he gazed upon her, the Idiot felt something very strange deep inside him, in a place he didn't know he had. It was a feeling, but one he had never felt before. He didn't know what to call this feeling. All he knew was that the princess somehow caused it. And as he looked upon her pale form, looking helpless and lifeless in the firelight, he felt tears spill from his eyes. He rubbed them away with a sleeve. Crying wasn't going to save the Princess. He would have to think of something else.

He knew not how to help her. He looked skyward for an answer, but all he could see were stars. He had never seen so many. They all seemed to be crowding into this small section of sky, just so they could look down upon her and drink in her beauty; as if by so doing their light would shine brighter.

He looked back down, upon her face, hands and arms, and saw that even the firelight seemed to delight in dancing on her skin, caressing her with its golden light. He wanted to kiss her. But he dared not.

The Idiot was used to people making fun of him, calling him names like...well...Idiot, and he had stayed away from them in his round, brick house. He couldn't remember the last time he had kissed or been kissed by anyone.

So he had come to know feelings that were not so nice, like loneliness and sadness and forgetfulness. But what he was feeling now was different from any feeling he had ever known.

Slowly and softly, he stroked her hair. Then he jumped back, expecting her to awaken and be annoyed with him.

But she did not awaken.

So he leaned forward and kissed her. Her lips were cold, as if she were dead. He was overcome with grief.

"Nooooooo," he cried. "Not dead. Don't be dead, Princess."

Suddenly, the air about him tingled. A purple light began to pulse and bathe the Princess's skin. It seemed to come from within her, but the Idiot soon realized that it came from a crystal amulet that hung around her neck. It was glowing and rhythmically pulsing like a beating heart. Color returned to the princess's cheeks. She opened her eyes.

What greeted her was a dirty, beggar-like creature, with shredded clothes and cuts and scratches on his skin. His hair was wiry, springing outwards from a head that looked down upon her full of concern.

She knew that the person she saw, despite his appearance, had probably come there to help her. He was on her side of the ring of fire, so that was a good sign. And beneath the dirt and the blood she could see that he was handsome, in a peculiar sort of way. "Are you my hero?" she asked softly.

The Idiot put a grin on his face.

Seeing his big, goofy smile, the princess smiled back. Then, the Idiot clapped his hands and began capering about with joy. "I'm so happy," he said. "I thought you were dead!"

"Thank you for saving me," she said, smiling so sweetly that the Idiot thought he would either melt or explode. "Tell me, please, kind Sir, where is the evil Witch?"

"She's over there," he replied and pointed beyond the flames.

The Princess stopped smiling and became suddenly afraid. "You mean you didn't kill her? What kind of hero are you?"

"The kind that doesn't kill little old ladies, I guess", the Idiot said.

"Quick," she said urgently, "take this." She lifted the amulet from around her neck and

handed it to him. "Keep it safe."

"What is it?"

"She must never get her hands on it. It's the only hope we have of defeating her."

"How does it work?"

"When you have a problem, you think about a solution, and the amulet will make it happen."

"I don't think I should. I'm not too good at thinking. You would be much better than me."

'But you are the one that saved me. Take it. I trust you to do the right thing."

"I shouldn't."

"Pleeeeze," she begged.

"OK," he said, not wanting to disappoint her, and he leaned his head forward as she put the crystal amulet about his neck. He already knew what to do, but now it didn't seem like a silly idea. "Follow me, Princess."

"But what are we going to do about the fire?"

"Well, I got this bird poop protector; the Witch thinks it's a wand, but lately it's been catching an awful lot of water which, maybe, it wants to get rid of."

The Idiot struggled with the umbrella at first. He tried squeezing it, then he tried to shake it, but nothing worked. He was just about to give up when suddenly, the crystal amulet about his neck began to glow and pulsate once more.

The umbrella started turning. As it turned, water began to fly from it. Though the canopy had been burned away, water flowed from holes in the umbrella's metal struts. The faster it turned, the more the water poured. It was like an over-size sprinkler.

Water hissed as flames turned it into steam, so that a thick vapor rose up about them. It also created a wet, soggy path through the fire; the Princess grabbed the Idiot's waist as he followed it.

When they suddenly found themselves safely on the other side of the ring of fire, the flames disappeared altogether. As the mist began to clear, they could see vague shapes begin to emerge.

Then they saw what they did not want to see.

Changes

Suddenly, the hideous, hairy Witch was revealed once more, in all her dirty, raggedy ugliness.

"At last! At long last you no longer have the protection of the 'ring of fire'," she crowed. "Thank you so much, Idiot. You have managed to do what I could not. You have freed this pretty young thing, with such a pretty thing around her neck. Now it shall be mine!"

She looked at the Princess, who was behind the Idiot. "Oh, no my dear; you can't hide. You belong to me now, as well as that certain precious something that we both know you have."

"Leave the princess alone!" the Idiot demanded, and he blocked the Witch from going any further.

"Fool. Idiot! And what do you suppose you can do? Why do you think I chose you in the first place? It certainly wasn't for your brains. I needed someone stupid enough to risk his life for a pretty girl and to bring me my prize. So, give it to me now!" She outstretched her hand.

"Give you what?" the Idiot asked.

"I don't suppose you know what I'm talking about, Idiot, but the Princess does, don't you?"

"Do you mean the amulet?" the princess asked." At the very mention of the name, the old Witch's eyes lit up with a greedy glow. "I don't have that anymore. I don't know where it is."

"Oh yes you do," the Witch contradicted. "I saw it myself. It was the last thing your father did before he left you in that accursed fire. He put it around your neck. Now give it to me at once, before I strangle you with it!" she spat.

"But I told you I don't have it."

"Liar!" The witch screeched hysterically.

"She doesn't; I do," said the Idiot.

The Princess couldn't believe what the Idiot had just said. "Why did you tell her?" she asked in a hoarse whisper.

"He's doing precisely what any idiot would, and now he will give me what I want." said the Witch as she waved her wand menacingly.

"Why are you waving that tree?"

The Witch looked at the wand in her hand. As she did so, it quickly began to change shape. First it became a twig which grew bigger and bigger, until it grew into a branch that got thicker and longer; then it became a trunk with lots of other branches growing off it. The Witch couldn't hold it

any longer and it fell to the ground. Roots began to grow from the base of the trunk and burrow into the earth. She jumped back with a yelp.

"No matter," she said, "I have other powers."

"Of course you do," said the Idiot, "and you want to use them to do *good*. I know you are a kind, caring person really, not mean. You don't have to be horrible. I think your daughter would like to know you as you really are."

Suddenly, a strange expression came over the old Witch's face. "No-one has ever spoken to me like that before," she said.

"But it will not be the last time. You have the power to turn wickedness and mischief into love. Your daughter needs you, whether you choose to believe it or not".

Like a quick snail, leaving behind a silver trail, a tear slid down her cheek. "But how did you know?" she asked.

"No one can be completely mean," the Idiot answered. "It's not too late, you know," he said.

"Yes it is," the Witch said sadly. "I fear that my daughter will never understand."

The Idiot took the Princess by the hand and led her to the old Witch. "Tell her now," he said.

"What are you doing?" the Princess asked. "I'm confused. Tell me what?" Then she leaned in close to the Witch and looked deep into her eyes. "Oh my Great Gorilla!" she cried. "Mummy?"

"I'm afraid so," the Witch confessed.

"But how can this be?" She turned to the Idiot. "And how did you know?"

"Well, you do look like each other," he replied.

"How can you say that? She's so UGLY!"

"Only on the outside," the Idiot said.

"Gee, thanks," said the Witch.

The Princess was unconvinced. "Frankly, I don't believe her. I don't trust her either. How is it possible to change from being a nasty, horrible, old witch so quickly?"

"I was not always nasty," the Witch said. "Besides, if you know that people can change into someone horrible, then you must believe that they can change back."

"Well, I am grateful that my hero rescued me from your nasty spell." the princess said. "But it was no thanks to you."

"But you don't understand, dear, I didn't put you under that spell."

"Well, if not you, then who?" she asked in a disbelieving tone.

"Your father, of course."

"That's crazy! My father can't make spells. That would mean that he was a..."

"...a wizard, yes."

"My father is no wizard!"

"If a mother can be a witch then, surely, a father can be a wizard. There is magic in every one of us, dear daughter. Even your friend here has a little magic in him." She gestured towards the Idiot.

"Well," the Princess said haughtily. "If that is true then why would my father put me in that place and cast a spell over me? He is a kind man. He wouldn't hurt me."

"Why don't we ask him?" offered the Idiot.

Just then the crystal about the Idiot's neck began to glow.

"I didn't cast a spell on you to hurt you," said a deep voice. "I did it to protect you."

They were amazed to see that the wand, which had become a tree, was now turning into a man. The tree's roots withdrew from the ground, twisting into feet and legs. Its branches and twigs formed two sinewy arms. Leaves stretched and stranded themselves into long, silver hair.

Finally, an old man stood before them.

Happy Family

"Daddy!" the Princess cried.

"Yes," the Wizard said. "It's me."

"But I don't understand. Why did you put me to sleep inside that horrible ring of fire?"

"Because I knew the only way I could protect you from the Witch was to build a wall around you, of the only thing that witches fear most: fire."

"But why didn't you keep the amulet, and use it against her."

"I didn't know how. I wasn't smart enough to find out how it worked. Your friend here is the only one who has been able to figure out how to use it properly".

"I didn't figure out nothin'," said the Idiot.

"Yes you did. You discovered that the amulet's power was to do good, not evil. And you saw the good in people that others don't see, even in her," the Wizard said. Then he turned to the Witch.

"You know, I didn't even need to protect our daughter. You wouldn't have been able to figure out how to use that amulet in a million years."

"Oh really?" Snorted the Witch

"Of course not," said the Wizard.

"I would have figured it out, because I'm smarter than you."

"Oh no you're not. Even the Idiot is smarter than you."

"Pipe down!"

"I will not pipe down," replied the Wizard. "You've been wrong ever since I have known you."

"Which is obviously too long. The only time I

was wrong was when I married you!" snapped the Witch.

"Me too!"

"Stop! Stop! Stop!" the Princess cried as she stepped in between them. "Don't you realize that this is a good thing? I have finally got both my parents back, and I am not asleep, and there is no fire, and I have just met with my true hero."

"Have you?" the Idiot asked, looking about him. "Who's that?"

"You, of course!"

The Idiot blushed.

"And you know what happens when princesses meet their heroes?"

"Er, no."

"The hero has to marry her."

"Oh."

"Is that all you've got to say?" she asked.

"OH!" He exclaimed when the full meaning of what she said finally sunk in. "But you don't want to marry me, Princess."

"Why ever not?" she asked. "Why wouldn't I want to marry the man that saved me?"

"Well," said the Idiot, "if we get married, that means we have to kiss."

"I thought you'd never ask," she said, throwing her arms around his neck and locking her lips onto his.

But their kiss was interrupted by a galloping sound, as if a herd of cattle were heading their way. All four of them hurriedly took cover behind a tree. Then they cautiously looked out from behind its trunk.

They saw a great cloud of dust, but not what made it. The whatever-it-was had almost passed them by before the dust cloud began to clear.

Now they could make out the shapes within it.

Broken Spells

They were surprised at what they saw, but they were not afraid. It was the 'shuffling people' from inside the castle, but they were no longer shuffling. They were running wild and free, their faces filled with joy.

"Hello," the Idiot called, stepping from behind the tree with the Princess and her parents. The shuffling people saw them and came to a halt.

"Hello there," said the whiney one, in a voice that was now pleasing to the ear.

"I see you found the Princess," the soft spoken one said. "*And* you woke her up."

"She's really pretty," said the girl. "You look good together."

"What happened?" asked the Idiot. "How did you break the Witches spell?"

"They didn't," the Witch said. "I released them from it. Since you showed me my good self, being mean just doesn't feel right anymore. Being nice feels so much better."

For a moment, the shuffling people were afraid to see the old Witch again. "It's OK," she reassured them. "My days of casting spells are over. I'm very sorry for any inconvenience I may have caused," she said apologetically.

"That's easy for you to say," said the one who smelt bad.

Then one of the shuffling people said to the Idiot, "we don't know how you managed it, but thank you for doing whatever it was you did." The voice belonged to the stuffy, impatient man, but there was now laughter in it.

"Thank you," they all chorused together. Then

they were running again. It was surprising to see how much ground they covered so quickly, and it wasn't long before they were out of sight.

"Well," said the Wizard. "I think it's also time for us to go."

The Witch smiled at him and took him by the hand. "Ready when you are, dear," she softly said. The Idiot noticed that the Witch had become less ugly. For one thing, the wart had disappeared from the end of her nose and her hair looked a lot cleaner and untangled. 'People are a lot nicer on the outside when they are good on the inside,' he thought.

Suddenly, there was a flash of lightening; in it, the Witch and the Wizard disappeared.

Welcome Home

The Princess smiled at the Idiot. "It's time for us to go too," she said.

"To where?" asked the Idiot.

"I don't know," answered the Princess. "All I do know is that I don't want to be here."

"Why don't you come back with me to my house?" he asked.

"Where is that?"

"On the other side of the waterfall," he replied.

"I don't know where that is," said she.

"Neither do I," he said gloomily.

"Look," she cried, "the amulet is glowing."

Sure enough, the amulet throbbed with a purple light. "I've got an idea," said the Idiot. "Maybe the bird poop protector can help."

"How?" asked the Princess.

"Well, it used up all the water inside it by putting out the ring of fire, so I think that it must be thirsty."

"I would never have thought of that," she said.

Then his umbrella began to twist and writhe in his hand; tugging at him as if trying to steer him in a particular direction. The Idiot tightened his grip and allowed it to lead him.

As they travelled back through the wilderness of the Witches domain, the sun rose up over distant hills as if to smile on their journey. Eventually, after many miles, the umbrella led them back through the tunnel to the waterfall.

It didn't matter that the umbrella no longer had a canopy with which to keep them dry. They laughed as the cascading water showered them.

Their shoes made squelching noises for many miles, but by the time they got back to the Idiot's place they were dry. He never did get to the shop to buy jam for his bread, but by now it was no longer breakfast time; he would just have to make dinner instead; 'dinner for two,' he thought happily.

At last he saw the familiar sight of his home, which made him even happier. He had opened the front gate and they were about to pass through it, when they saw a group of four lads coming towards them.

"Well, look who we've got here," one of them said. "If it ain't that gaumless twit, the Idiot."

"My oh my," said another, "get a load of what he's carrying. Look at that beat up old umbrella. Don't he know that ain't going to stop the rain?"

Their voices were familiar. He had heard them many times. The last time was when they nearly ran him down in their car.

"Wait a minute," another of them said, in a

sinister voice. "Who's that pretty lady with him?" Then he spoke to the Princess, "You don't want to get too close to him, my lovely. He's just an idiot, hasn't got two brain cells to rub together. He's not what you would call smart. He wouldn't know how to make a pretty little thing like you happy. You should come with us."

The Princess could take no more of this and stepped forward. They saw the anger in her face as she glared at each of them in turn. "I'll have you know that this man is my hero. And not just mine. He defeated an evil witch and broke her spells and freed a lot of grateful people. It took courage and intelligence. So it's not surprising that none of you were there to help!"

"You must mean someone else. He couldn't think his way out of bed," another one sneered.

"He uses his brain differently, and it is just as well. Some situations call for a special type of intelligence. But I guess you wouldn't know about that. What's more disturbing, is why you feel the need to be so horrible. If you think it makes you look clever, you're wrong. Really, anyone who has to put someone else down just to make themselves feel good, is not someone I want to be around!" And with that she turned her back on them, hooked her arm into the Idiot's and they walked through the gate and up the winding path to his front door.

The four lads had no answer for that. All they could do was watch with open mouths and dumb expressions on their faces. As he turned the door handle, the Idiot winked and said "Welcome home, Princess."

"I like the sound of that," she replied.

Then they went indoors together, and began to live happily ever after.

~ The End ~

Or not . . . ?

The Idiot Song

When I'm thinking what I say
And put words in a sentence
People shake their heads and say
'That don't make no sense.'

> Chorus
> Coz, I'm an idiot, a clueless clot.
> I never remember what I forgot,
> Or what is what. I've lost the plot.
> I try my best not to think a lot,
> Coz it hurts my brain.
> I don't even know my name.

When I goes out for a walk
I turn to see what way I'm going.
Then I walk backwards, then the other way
And I do some to-ing and fro-ing
> Chorus
I likes to swim, very, very far
But I don't take time to think.
Then I gets tired and I have to stop,
And so I start to sink
> Chorus
Some people they make fun of me
Some people think I'm mad
Some people think I'm lazy
Some people think I'm bad
But I likes nearly everyone
Until they makes me sad
But then I can't remember
A single word they said
> Chorus

The Idiot Dance

Arms out to sides, left arm low, right arm high.

1.   Step forward with right foot
      and slide left foot behind right.

2.   Repeat

3.   Repeat

4.   Step onto right foot. Hop on right foot.

Arms out to sides, right arm low, left arm high.

1.   Step forward with left foot
      and slide right foot to behind left.

2.   Repeat

3.   Repeat

4.   Step onto left foot. Hop onto left foot.

Keep repeating until you are really, really tired.

Acknowledgements

A great big thank you to my family for their support; in particular, my sons Blake and Myles for asking for this book to be read, long after any obligation to do so had expired; to my mother, Elaine, for always being in my corner and making things possible; and to my wife, Karen, for slaying dragons in the real world, enabling me to spend more time in my imaginary ones.

A great big thank you to Karen Moss for her insistence that the Idiot should be released from the prison of my computer, and for her invaluable editing, proof-reading, and continuity inconsistency spotting skills, and friendship. And a big thank you to Suzannah Lockyer, my lifelong friend and word conspirator.

And a great big thank you, to you dear reader. I hope you have been well rewarded. I have certainly enjoyed the possibility of pleasing you.

EXTRACT
HOUSE

Other books...

...have been written and are lurking in this machine somewhere.

I will try and coax them out with promises of fame and notoriety. If that doesn't work, I'll enter the jungle of my computer myself, machete in hand, and valiantly fight to keep them from the dungeons of oblivion.

So keep an eye open for them, especially books whose main character begins with the letter 'R'.

Errol

Errol Dawson

December, 2013
Auckland, New Zealand

Made in the USA
Middletown, DE
26 September 2024

61495800R00060